iN THE GARAGE

iN THE GARAGE
Alma Fullerton

Red Deer PRESS

PUBLISHED BY

Red Deer Press
A Fitzhenry & Whiteside Company
1512, 1800—4 Street S.W.
Calgary, Alberta, Canada T2S 2S5
www.reddeerpress.com

CREDITS

Edited for the Press by Peter Carver
Copyedited by Kirstin Morrell
Cover and text design by Erin Woodward
Cover images courtesy iStock
Printed and bound in Canada by Friesens for Red Deer Press

ACKNOWLEDGMENTS

Financial support provided by the Canada Council. We acknowledge the financial support of the Government of Canada through the Book Publishing Industry Development Program (BPIDP) for our publishing activities.

NATIONAL LIBRARY OF CANADA CATALOGUING IN PUBLICATION

Fullerton, Alma
in the garage / Alma Fullerton.
ISBN 0-88995-371-6
i. Title.
PS8611.U45I58 2006   jC813'.6   C2006-904889-4

To Jessica and Chantale. I hope you always remember to love yourselves. You're both worth it.

Thanks to my ducky pals: Anne Marie Pace, Cassandra Whetstone, Shelly Becker, Katy Duffield, Tanya Seale, and Kristy Dempsey. Special thanks to Mike Banka.

Part One

Acceptance of prevailing standards often means we have no standards of our own.

–Jean Toomer

Barbara Jean Belanger

There'll always be shit that happens in your life that'll make you wonder what the hell God was thinking when he made humans.

I'm reading the *Weird World News* across the kitchen table from Dad and Nan as they argue about Nan's cribbage score.

Nan's swearing in French and tells him, "I got a thirty-two hand and dere's nutting you can do about it but lose."

Then Dad goes, "Put your glasses on, dearest Maman, and count again—because there's no possible way you can get a thirty-two hand in cribbage when the highest is twenty-nine."

Nan clunks the back of Dad's head with the empty card box. "Don't talk back to your elders." Then she goes on in French about how she didn't raise no rude kids and how Dad must have been brainwashed while he was in the army.

I hold my paper higher and snicker, thinking that's what Dad's always ragging on me about—except for the army part—and that's when I see the story.

"Listen to this," I say. Nan and Dad stop fighting. "Some scientists in Japan invented a new kind of gum. By chewing it, your boobs can get eighty percent bigger. Ha!" They laugh and I go on, "You know, the guys are going to majorly dis me and tell me I need gum that'll make my boobs shrink but they'll love this story—especially Alex." I look at Dad and Nan. They're staring at me with their mouths hanging open.

And suddenly I feel like I've been slapped.

Alex is gone, and I find myself lost in a thick fog of emotion where

    I'm left

        Gasping

           For

              Air.

Alex Fitzgerald's Journal

Haunted

I'm haunted by a secret
that will eat away my insides,
until I'm empty
and my life
disintegrates into
nothingness.

BJ

What happened to Alex Fitzgerald is one of those things.

The closest I've come to going to church is driving around the frigging cars that block our driveway when there are people in the church across the street. So standing here, trying to give my best friend's eulogy makes me want to scream louder than a cheap guitar when you stand too close to the amp.

Everyone's gawking at me like I'm some kind of circus freak. They're staring at *me*, at my scar, at my blotch, picking out all that's wrong with me, and I'm numb.

I'm listening to the creaking seats, the coughs, and the *eh-hems* echoing off the church ceiling. I'm standing here, in front of God, the priest and everybody listening to

EVERY
SINGLE
AMPLIFIED
BREATH,
of everyone in front of me, unable to say a
Goddamn word about the guy who was my best
friend for eight years. All I can do is stand here
silent, and think how it all began.

Alex's Journal

Alone

Surrounded by friends,
I feel
Alone.

None of them
is like me.

Tormented
by what I am,
and confronted by
what I want to be.

BJ

If God made us in his image does that mean
he's screwed up too?

I'm just a little kid and it's early in the morning.
I'm plunked in the backseat of my mother's red
Honda. Rain drums on the roof. It sounds like
music. I listen and watch raindrops dance in the
parking lot. Rain ploink, ploink, ploinks faster
against the roof. It's dripping down the window,
turning everything outside blurry.

My mom rests her head against the steering
wheel. A line of her cigarette smoke wiggles back
and tickles my nose. I sneeze. She jerks straight up,
swears, and bang, bang, bangs her hands against
the wheel, three times—I count them.

"Mommy, you okay?" I whisper.

"Shut up." She turns around and smacks me. I
whimper and hide my face behind my hands.

"Stop your goddamn bawling. You're so stupid. Don't you know everyone hates a crybaby?" She turns and shakes me so my head bangs against the seat and I bawl harder. "I told you to stop your goddamn crying!"

She shoves open her door and gets out. "I can't stand to look at your ugly face anymore!" She slams the door and walks away with fast, long steps. She doesn't look back—not once. She just leaves me there—alone and sniffling in the backseat of her car.

I'm just a little kid and I watch my mother race away from me through a lopsided world of water.

And the rain keeps ploink, ploink, ploinking on the roof of her red Honda.

★ ★ ★ ★

The sun shines through the car's window and wakes me up from my nap. I look outside for my mom but don't see her. Instead, there's a lady standing outside the car looking in at me. She waves her hands and goes, "Where's your mommy?"

I shrug. She crunches her face up like Mommy does sometimes when she's mad at me or Daddy; then she goes into the store.

I watch the store doors opening and closing. Every time I check for Mommy but she's not coming. It's hotter and my hair feels wet so I wipe my forehead with my shirtsleeve.

The lady from before comes back with a cart full of groceries and stops and looks at me funny. "Open the door, sweetie," she says.

But I won't. Daddy tells me never to talk to people I don't know. I don't know this lady. "Come on, honey, open the door. I won't hurt you," she goes again.

But I still won't, so she runs away and brings back a man. He's big and looks scary. I pull my coat up over my face so I can't see them. I hear them banging, but if I can't see them, they can't see me either and maybe they'll go away.

It's getting even hotter under here, so I take off my raincoat again and look outside for Mommy.

Mommy's still not there, but that lady is. Her face is wet and red, and her eyes are puffy.

I have to pee and I'm thirsty, but I won't unlock the door 'cause now there are so many people running around the car, they're scaring me.

I peek in my snack bag and pull out a juice box. The straw is hard to get in the hole and when it finally goes in, purple juice squirts all over the seat and carpet. Mommy will be mad. She'll probably spank me and that makes me scareder, but I won't cry. Mommy said no one likes a crybaby.

Soon there are policemen outside the car asking me to unlock the door, but I won't 'cause I don't know those policemen either. I still have to go pee and I can't hold it anymore. I wet my pants 'cause there's no potty and that'll make Mommy madder. That makes me even scareder and I try really hard not to cry. But I can feel my bottom lip moving and my eyes get blurry and everything outside gets lopsided like Mommy did when she left. I wipe away the lopsided people 'cause as long as I don't cry, Mommy will come back.

The policeman outside pulls out a long, flat thing and the front door unlocks. He leans in and pulls me out. Daddy's car drives up. He jumps out and grabs me from the policeman's arms. Even though my pants are wet and I spilled juice in the car he hugs me close, kisses my head, and says, "I can't believe she did this to you."

And I wonder three things. Who is *she?* What did she do? And when is Mommy coming back to see I'm not a crybaby anymore?

* * * *

It's a few days later and I sit in a chair on the front porch eating some peanut butter crackers and kicking the air with my feet. I keep looking up the road to see if Mommy's coming home. But I never see her. A cab pulls into the driveway and I run to it calling, "Mommy, Mommy, Mommy!"

Daddy comes out of the house, but it's not Mommy getting out of the cab. It's Nan.

Nan is good too 'cause she brings cookies and toys. This time she doesn't have cookies or toys. She has a lot of suitcases and a kitty. She hugs me tight and hands me the kitty. "Pour toi," she goes. "Une petite amie." She's soft so I hug her hard and pull her to my face. She whines and scratches me with her claws. Then Nan says, "Be gentle."

But instead of being gentle I go, "Stop whining, you stupid kitty, no one likes a crybaby," and drop it on the grass. "I don't want to look at your ugly face anymore," and I stomp back to my chair to wait for Mommy.

Daddy and Nan look at each other and frown. "Maman," he says, "thank you for coming." He hugs her, whispers something in her ear, and grabs her bags. "BJ, Nan is going to stay with us. Isn't that great?"

"Will she make cookies?" I ask.

"All de time," Nan goes, "and you can help."

"Now?" I say.

"Sure!" Nan tells me. "Come on." I look down the road one more time, jump up and go into the kitchen with Nan. The kitty follows me and plays with my loose shoelace. I think she's not so ugly after all and I think I'll name her Sunny 'cause it's sunny outside today and she makes me happy like the sun does. I pick her up and kiss her head gently 'cause she's not crying anymore.

Alex's Journal

Flawed

It's better to be flawed outside,
like BJ,
than to be flawed inside
like me,
because right off she knows
what to expect from people.
Right now,
I don't even know
what to expect from
myself.

BJ

*True friends are gifts from God. Don't turn
them away.*

"Ugly, ugly, ugly!"

It's third grade and Brian and Darren—fifth-
grade Booger-Bullies—push me around. Their
jackets swing as they shove me between each
other, back and forth, back and forth. I'm getting
dizzy. I trip and scrape my hand along the hot
pavement. I won't cry though.

Other kids surround us and join in with,
"Ugly, ugly, ugly."

I jump to my feet and glare at Brian and
Darren. "I may be ugly, but you're so slow in the
head your mothers must have screwed turtles!"
Some of the kids laugh. That makes Booger-
Bullies' faces scrunch up like they're sucking
lemons. They push me hard against the wall and
the bricks hurt my back.

I turn to run, but a ball whacks the wall beside me. I turn the other way and another ball slams against the wall. I move right—*thwack*. Left—*thwack*. I can't run away and they throw the balls at me. They sting my arms and legs and leave red marks.

But I won't cry.

I can't cry, 'cause everyone hates a crybaby.

Suddenly this skinny new kid runs past all the other kids, like he's some kind of king. The perfect kids watch him grinning, as he tears toward me.

New Kid is right in front of me. I flinch thinking he's going to plow me in the face. Instead, he spins so fast rocks spray around his shoes. Then he yells, "Stop it!"

Brian steps forward and goes, "Why don't you make me, wimpy?" He chucks a ball at New Kid, who reaches out and catches it faster than a NHL goalie grabs a slap-shot. Then New Kid chucks it back and hits Brian in the head.

"How do you like it?" New Kid says back.

Brian takes a swing at New Kid's face but the kid stops the punch and plows Brian in the chin. Brian falls backwards.

"Anyone else want to try?" New Kid asks, stepping forward. They all shake their heads and leave. New Kid turns around, "You okay?"

"Sure," I say.

He sticks his hand out, "Hi, my name is Alex Fitzgerald. I just moved here with my dad."

I shake his hand. "BJ Belanger."

"Want to play with me?" he asks.

I nod, and since that day Alex and I have been best friends.

* * * *

It's my eighth birthday party. It's just me, Dad, Nan, and Alex. Alex leans forward and balances on his seat when Dad brings in my gift.

"Well, BJ, since you told us to surprise you, Alex, Nan, and I put our heads—and wallets— together and came up with this. Hope you like it." Dad hands me a big box, wrapped in blue paper.

I'm unwrapping it all dainty like, trying to save the paper.

Alex bounces on his chair. He taps the table. He hums and groans.

I smirk. I'm unwrapping the present too slow for him and I know it. I go, "Maybe we should eat our cake first?"

"Ahhhh!" Alex jumps from his seat and runs around the table so he's standing over me. "Open it! Will ya just hurry up and open it?"

Dad, Nan, and I laugh; then I tear off the wrapping paper. It's a brown box. I pop open the box and there's this silver video camera inside.

Nan goes, "It was Alex's idea."

"You like it?" Alex says.

"We know you don't like to be in front of the camera, so we thought maybe you'd like to be behind one," Dad says.

I can't think of anything to say. A video camera.

"I . . . I thought you'd like it," Alex goes, when I don't say anything.

I jump from my seat, put the video camera on the table and hug him tight. "I love it. It's the best present ever."

Alex's Journal

Escape

For my tenth birthday more than anything
I wanted a guitar,
but Dad insisted on a basketball net.

For my tenth birthday more than anything
I wanted a guitar,
and BJ knew Dad wouldn't buy it.

So on my tenth birthday,
BJ took her own birthday money,
and used IT to buy me
my first guitar.

On my tenth birthday,
BJ gave me
my escape.

BJ

Silence between two people can be awkward, but silence between true friends can be comforting.

Even now, in eleventh grade, Alex and I always sit together for lunch. Neither of us tries to keep our conversation going, because we've been friends so long we can just be happy being bored together.

I really don't know how that happened. We're so different. He's the kind of kid everyone wants to be—good-looking, talented, great at sports, rich, and everyone's friend—and, well, I'm not.

Maybe we're friends because neither of us have our real mothers around. Or maybe it's because we both have creative sides—him with music and me with movie-making—and that makes us understand each other.

But I think it's mostly because he's never allowed his "all that" to creep into his head like most people do. Alex has always, and will always be Alex. Hanging with him makes a person feel the same as lazing around in an overstuffed chair, wearing a well-worn pair of pajamas.

Usually when I'm not with Alex, or hiding behind the lens of my video camera, I want to fold myself up and disappear into the trashcan behind the school like a 'burn note' written by another girl.

Alex's Journal

Expectations

My Dad tells me,
"Son, you have to have
the highest point average in a game
or the scouts will pick someone else."

He says,
"I expect to see
all A's on your report card.
B's are not good enough."

He says,
"Look to your future, son.
You can have the best.
The best wife.
The best kids.
Nothing but the best."

And when I think about
everything he expects from me,
my stomach knots up
and jumps up to my throat,
because I know
I can't be the person
he wants me to be.

And when I don't live up to
his expectations,
I shrink so small
he can no longer see me
when I'm standing
right in front
of him.

BJ

*Vanity is like a drug—the more you take of
it, the more brain cells you fry.*

I yank open my locker and a note falls out. I stoop
to snatch it off the tiles and stuff it deep into my
pocket. If Alex sees it, he'll get all freaked out
about how he wishes people would just lay off me.

I get so many of these notes, I don't have to
open it to know what it says, but later when Alex is
in a different class I do.

That note says, *Alex only likes you because he
wants to work for the humane society.*

That note says, *How can Alex hold his food in
when he eats at the same table with you?*

That note says, *It can't be because he wants to
do a dog because you wouldn't be even a good lay
with a bag over your head.*

That note flattens me like a frog that has been
left in a glass container for two weeks without water.

But when I get to the end, that note makes me smile. I wonder if being pretty makes a person's head lose so many brain cells they can't spell anonymous.

Alex's Journal

Hugs from a Kid

While I'm playing my guitar
everything bad in my world
disappears,
and I feel like I do
when my four-year-old half-brother, Jacob,
comes to find me
just to hug me
for no reason.

BJ

Laughter can bandage wounds but it can't take away the sting.

In the school's hallway the guys and I talk about how we plan to become famous and die legends. Before I can tell them how I want to film an Oscar-winning movie, this perfect girl I don't know gawks at me.

She goes, "Ever hear of something called a diet? You look like a slob."

The guys shift their feet and stare at the ground.

I suck in a breath. "I can't go on a diet."

"Why not?" she asks.

"Because I have to eat lots and gain a ton of weight so when I fall down and die I'll leave a huge mark on the world."

The guys laugh, and relax. The girl huffs and stomps away—burned.

"All right, BJ!" Alex goes. He gives me a high-five. "You showed her."

"I did," I say, pretending what she said didn't bug me, but inside my soul is being smooshed every time her spiky high heels take a perfect step away from us.

Alex's Journal

Acting

BJ knows me so well,
I'm afraid sometimes
she can look deep into my eyes
and see my whole life is an act.
Just like I can look deep into her eyes,
and see that sometimes
she's acting too.

BJ

For some people, being accepted by their peers can mean the difference between life and death.

Alex and the guys like me for me. They aren't scared to be seen hanging with someone who wasn't made perfect. I meet them at the skate park and videotape them skateboarding. Rick slams the pavement trying to hang in the air. He jumps to his feet, flicks away the blood gushing out of his nose, and smiles at me. "Sick! You get that on tape?"

I give him a thumbs-up. He does a couple of ollies before hitting the ramp again.

Victoria and Rachel, two of our high school's queen bees, lean on the railings nearby. They flirt with the guys, squealing every time someone wipes out and bloodies up an arm or something. I zoom in on them and they smile and wave at the camera.

Standing near them, I play like they're my friends and I'm hanging with them like girls do. But even though neither of them has ever been nasty to me, I know that without the camera they'd totally ignore me. Because, to girls like them, I'm just an ugly blotch on the face of the world like the port-stain blotch on my face.

Alex's Journal

I'm Not an American Idol

Jacob follows me around
like I'm some kind of teen idol.
I want to slap him and tell him
that my life is so fucked up
he should find someone else
to idolize.

But then he rushes into the garage,
to show me a new string he learned to play
on the old acoustic guitar I gave him,
and I can't make myself tell him the truth.

Instead I wrap him tight in my arms
and close my eyes,
praying
he never has to deal with what
I'm dealing with.

BJ

It's amazing how something so little can make a person fill up inside.

The smell of flowers hangs in Alex's living room like a spring day. I close my eyes, take a deep breath, and imagine the sun on my face. It warms up my insides and I smile.

At first I can't see where the smell is coming from, but then I notice a vase in the corner with tiny, white flowers in it.

"They're lily of the valley," Alex's stepmom, Jen, says so suddenly I almost drop the vase.

"They smell nice."

Jen smiles. "Stay here for a minute. I'll be right back." She walks out of the room, leaving me alone.

A couple of minutes later, she comes back carrying some more lily of the valley. She brushes the hair out of my face and pins it back on one side with the flowers and a bobby pin. She smiles. "You're very pretty, you know?"

"Yeah, right." I roll my eyes, thinking she's just being nice.

"No, really, come see." She leads me to the hallway mirror.

The hair on my bad side is covering my birthmark so I can't see it. But the hair on my good side is pinned back, showing my face. I do look good. I turn sideways and glance again. From that angle, if I lost some weight I might even pass for one of Victoria's and Rachel's groupies.

Jen stands behind me grinning. When I smile at her reflection, I'm even prettier.

"Told you." She gives my shoulders a squeeze, and I wonder if this is what it feels like to have a mother around that loves you.

* * * *

We're ten and we're playing in the plastic pool in my back yard.

"I'm getting a new mom," Alex goes as he splashes down.

"Really?" I ask. "Cool!" I sit in the pool beside him.

"I guess."

"You don't like her?"

"It's not that; she's really nice," he says, "and pretty too. But she's not my mom, and you hear those stories about evil stepmothers and stuff. Maybe after they get married she'll turn mean."

"Those stories are fake," I go. "What's her name?"

"Jen."

"Jen is a good name for a mom," I tell him. "Not an evil stepmother name. You're lucky. I wish my dad would get married again."

"Yeah, I am lucky." He smiles. "Jen *is* a good name for a mom—my mom."

Alex's Journal

Proud of Me

Dad doesn't know
I hate basketball.
He doesn't know
I only play because
he comes to watch
with Jacob and Jen
and they all
cheer me on.

Dad cheers the hardest,
like I'm not the greatest
disappointment
in his life.

He yells over the crowd,
"Nice shot, son!"

He tells Jacob
"Someday, you might
be able to play ball
like your big brother."
And Jacob yells,
"Yay!"

Dad cheers
like he's actually
proud
of me.

BJ

Listening to a good singer can make you float inside. Listening to a bad one can make you cover your ears and run out of the room screaming.

I set up my video equipment in Alex's garage, so we can check out the clips I shot at the park. We mix their music into the background and make a dummy video. It sounds a little wonky at first, but works.

"You need a really good lead singer," I say.

"What's wrong with me?" Rick asks.

"You play a mean bass but you sing like a dying crow."

"BURNED!" Pete goes.

Rick squawks, then laughs because he knows it's true.

"Got an idea," Alex goes. He leaves and comes back later carrying several Cokes and a stack of signs.

"Let's split up and hang these up." He hands each of us a Coke and several signs.

Wanted Singer
Male or Female
Must like punk and Emo.
Auditions held at 7:00 pm Friday.
102 Queen Street.
IN THE GARAGE.

Alex's Journal

Some Days

After my games
Dad and I go out, alone.
On the days when I reach the
highest point average,
being with Dad can be like
flying.
But on the days when I have a
bad game,
Dad says things like,
"The coach should have pulled you."
Or, "You're going to have to step it up
if you want the scouts to look at you."
And being with him is worse than
drowning
in my own shit.

BJ

A good movie can pull you out of your life and put you into someone else's, and the more you step into someone else's life the more you can learn about yours.

I decide to film a documentary called *The Making of a Band*. In the garage the guys and I hang a sheet on the wall and set up a stage with lights.

"This will be great for promo," Alex goes, as he moves the last light into place.

He looks outside to see if anyone is coming. "Might as well practice while we wait."

"Hey, you guys are good." The first guy comes in. He wanders to the mike. "Y'all know any country?"

"Ah . . . no," Alex goes. "We're looking for a punk singer."

The guy nods his head and screams into the mike. He doesn't say nothing, he just screams until Alex stops him.

"Not that kind of punk," Alex goes. He leads the guy outside and brings back Victoria and Rachel.

"You trying out?" I ask.

"God, no." Rachel laughs. "We just want to watch."

I watch her hitting on Rick, wishing I was made so perfect I'd have guys eating out of the palm of my hand. I turn and see Victoria hit on Alex. A balloon grows in my throat until I swallow and look down to fiddle with my camera.

* * * *

Six more people answer our ad and they're so bad I figure I can send their clips to some kind of blooper show and make mega bucks.

As I film, one guy comes in dressed in an ostrich suit, thinking the ad said *Must like Punk and emus.*

When he leaves, Victoria asks, "Did you catch that, BJ? Did you get him on tape?"

"Oh yeah!" I go, and her, Rachel, and I laugh together. They high-five me and pat me on the back. I'm guessing that maybe they aren't as stuck-up as I thought because they're treating me just like one of their friends, and that makes my stomach whirl.

Alex's Journal

Invisible Shields

When Jacob plays in the yard
he's off in his own world,
surrounded by the
invisible shield
of childhood that
prevents him from getting hurt
by the evil things
in the real world.

More than ever,
I want that shield back.

BJ

Words tell lies. Actions tell truths. What you do can show another person exactly who you are.

It's Saturday, and I rush to Alex's place to tell the guys my *Weird News* for the week.

"Guess what I just read?" I barge into the garage. The guys stop playing to listen. "Some actor erased his nose using this new kind of makeup! He was gorgeous but now he doesn't have a nose!"

"What? His nose is totally gone?" Pete asks. "No way."

"Yeah, doctors rushed in and pumped his nose back out with a mini air hose. Anyhow, when the actor opens his mouth the air comes out and his nose disappears again! Talk about an airhead."

"Sick!" Rick goes. "Is he suing?"

"Big time." I nod.

"I'd sue too," Pete goes.

They get back to practicing and I'm filming for my doc when this kid from school walks in.

His real name is David something or other, but the kids at school just call him Faggot. He flips his blond shag out of his eyes and looks at me. "Hey," he goes. His smile warms me up inside and I can tell by the look on his face he's really into what the band is playing.

"You guys are awesome," David says when they finish their song. "You still looking for a singer?"

Rick puts down his bass and without looking at David goes, "Yes, but not you."

"What's wrong with me?" David asks. He clenches his fists by his side.

"You're a faggot." Rick steps toward David like he's ready to beat the shit out of him.

I zoom out and get them both on the cam.

"So?" David goes.

Rick moves up again and I wince. David doesn't know about Rick's freak-outs, or how he can be such a hotheaded asshole, so he doesn't back away and stares Rick down. I get the feeling he's not as wimpy as he looks and maybe he can clean the floor with Rick's ass, but Rick takes another step and David backs off.

Alex glances at Jacob, who's playing with a microphone, and gets himself between Rick and David. "Can you sing?" he asks David.

"I've been told so," David tells him.

"Jacob," Alex says. "Hand David that mike."

Jacob skips over and gives David the mike. Rick huffs and plunks himself in a chair.

David flicks on the mike and goes into this incredible unaccompanied ultra-soft Emo solo. His voice lifts me off the floor and makes the room spin. When he's done, he puts down the mike and looks up. For a few minutes even Rick shuts up.

"Holy sh . . . ," Pete looks at Jacob, and stops. "I think we need to have a group huddle."

I film David. He shifts his feet and sucks back a gulp of air. I turn my cam onto the huddle.

Rick eyes David, shakes his head, and loud enough for David to hear goes, "I'm not working with a fag."

David sighs and looks around. He sees me filming him and glares into the lens.

I feel like he's looking right through it and into me. So I turn it away and film the guys again.

Alex and Pete are trying to reason with Rick, saying things like, "But he's really, really good and we have to do what's best for the band."

But Rick gets madder, and kicks over a mike stand. It crashes against the floor, missing Jacob's head by about an inch. "If he comes in—I leave. I'm not going to be on stage in front of the whole school with a fucking fag. It's me or him. You choose." He sneers at David.

David leans against the wall, and finds something interesting to look at on the floor by his feet.

Alex and Pete look at each other, then at David—who is starting to head for the door. They look back at Rick, then at the overturned mike stand, and Jacob—who is now crying about almost being smacked in the head with the stand—then at each other again.

Pete asks David, "Can you play bass?"

David looks back from the door quickly and goes, "Yeah." He smirks at Rick. "Yeah—I can play bass."

"Fuck you all!" Rick spits at Alex, and slams his bass into its case. He looks directly at me and asks, "Did you get that, you pathetic, sorry-assed-face of a bitch?"

He glares into the lens. "Did you, you fucking loser? It will be great footage for your fucking doc-cuuuu-mentary. Don't you think?" He storms toward the garage door. "You'll all regret this. One day, I guarantee it—you'll regret it."

As the garage door slams behind him, it rips me straight out of my body, and whips me onto the floor. I let my camera drop to my lap. It films Jacob, wide-eyed and teary, clinging to Alex's waist. Alex stands in front of me, his face as white as the little dots on a snowy TV screen.

Alex's Journal

I Don't Understand

I don't understand
how people can be so
consumed with so much
hate or fear,
for something they
don't understand
they don't realize
what they are doing
at the time they are
doing it.

BJ

We think we choose our friends but they really choose us.

Later, I sit at my kitchen table. Alex walks around the room and he's making me dizzy. "What's up?" I ask.

He plunks down in a chair. "I don't know," he goes. "Mostly, it's what just happened. Rick has been our friend for a long time. But his temper has gotten so bad I don't feel like I can trust him anymore. I swear, I thought he was going to cream David for absolutely nothing—right in front of Jacob. That scared the shit out of me."

He gets up and starts pacing again. "Everything in my life is changing, BJ. It's coming at me all at once and I don't know what to do anymore."

I shift in my seat, but just listen.

"BJ?" He looks at me all serious like he's about to tell me something really terrible.

I'm afraid he's going to agree with Rick and everyone else. I'm afraid he'll tell me I'm a pathetic loser and that he doesn't want me hanging around him anymore. I'm afraid he'll leave me sitting alone in the room and never come back. I'm afraid to stay and want to bolt to make sure I'm the first one to leave. But instead of running, I look up to listen, because that's what best friends do.

His lips open but nothing comes out. "Never mind," he goes. "Let's just get out of here."

I slouch in the chair and let out the breath I didn't know I was holding.

Alex's Journal

I Wish I Could Tell Her

Normally, I can tell BJ
anything.
When I do she always knows how
to make me feel like
everything will be okay.

But this time,
I don't even think BJ
can give me that kind of
assurance.

And inside,
I'm screaming so loud
I get headaches.

BJ

In the war on low self-esteem a "burn" can
be the bomb that blows you apart.

At the beach a line of guys sit on the fence in
front of the girls' bathroom. They're hooting and
shoving each other. When I get closer I hear what
they're doing and freeze. No way I can walk by
that line.

I watch Rachel strut by them. The guys call,
"TEN." She looks at them and grins.

Victoria stands tall and prances by.

The guys hoot again and call, "TEN and a half."

She giggles and spins around, modeling her
new bikini. She sees me and stops mid-spin. She
watches as I stand here—a freak—leaning against
the garbage can in my baggy men's shorts and
oversized T-shirt, petrified to pass that stupid line-
up. She stands in front of me, raising her eyebrow
in a dare for me to pass by.

I take a deep breath, stare at my feet, and hustle past the judges, hoping I won't be around long enough to hear my score.

"Minus TEN!" the boys' voices echo through the bathroom, and wrap around my neck choking me.

"Whoof, whoof!" Rachel and Victoria make dog noises as they enter the room, then break into hysterics.

I find the nearest stall, and hide there until it's too dark outside for anyone to see me leave.

Alex's Journal

Lectures

Pete, David, BJ, and I
go to the Spit and get trashed.
Dad's sitting on the couch waiting
for me when I crawl through the door.

He stands up and helps me off the floor,
and goes into one of his long lectures.
"You're too young to be wasted."

He sits me in a kitchen chair.
"Alex, you have to set
a good example for Jacob.
You know he idolizes you.
What if he woke up
and came downstairs
and saw you like this?"

He grabs the garbage pail
as I start to heave.
"These kids you're hanging
around with,
they're a bad influence."

He hands me a towel
to wipe my face.
"I know you've been friends
with BJ a long time
but she's not your kind of girl.
You should find someone
prettier—smarter—richer."

I can't stand listening to him
anymore.
So I pull myself up and
force myself past him
and up the stairs, leaving
him alone in the kitchen
with his mouth flapping—
right in the middle
of his long
lecture.

BJ

When you're little you think dandelions are flowers; it's not until you're grown up that you think they're weeds. The dandelions never changed. Your standards did.

Nan wraps her arms around me and goes, "Let's go shopping at the mall. We'll get you a new dress for de dance dis evening."

"It's okay, Nan," I go, "I don't need a new dress."

"Every girl needs a new dress. Up! Let's go." Nan taps my shoulders and grabs her purse. "It'll be fun."

I snort. Shopping with Nan at the mall is as much fun as sticking bamboo shoots under your fingernails—not that I've ever done that or anything—but I'm figuring it's not very fun.

"You should go," Dad says. "Get something nice. Break a few hearts tonight." He kisses my forehead and hands me forty bucks.

"Come on, *debout*. Up. Up." She motions with her arms. "Time to get out of dat La-Z-Boy and out in de real world."

With a moan I roll myself out of the chair, switch off the tube, and follow her to the car.

* * * *

The mall is far from "de real world" despite what Nan says. The mall is the home of the Queen Bees and all of their perfectly shaped friends. It's where they feel most comfortable—it's their zone, their competition place. You go to the mall and they know who you were with, which stores you shopped in, what you bought, and how much it costs.

If none of those things lives up to their standards, they spread it through their "cell phone hive" and within hours you're the laughing stock of the whole school.

I slouch behind Nan, hoping none of them sees me.

"How about dis one?" Nan holds up a bold brown and yellow striped dress. It's probably the ugliest thing I've seen in my life and the expression on my face must say so, because Nan frowns and looks at the dress again. "Non," she goes, "non, it's not right. It's not you."

She's right. It's not me. There's nothing here that's me but me and I just want to get out of here. It's bad enough being in Target but being in the oversized section with your grandmother is social suicide. I shift my feet and look around.

"How 'bout this one?" Nan smiles. "It's perfect."

I was wrong about the last dress. It wasn't the ugliest dress I've ever seen—this one is. If Nan thinks this dress is me she's either got bad taste or she's majorly dissing me. I figure it's a bad taste thing and I don't want to hurt her feelings so I go, "Yeah—okay." I grab it and head for the cash registers.

"BJ, you need to try it on." Nan catches up to me.

"Why?" I go. "It's my size. It's fine. It'll fit."

"But things are sized differently. You need to try it on. If it doesn't fit, we'll have to come back."

I am *not* coming back, so I head for the change room. This thing has layers. These layers flop all over the place so I can't tell which hole is for my head and which is for my arms. This thing is not only *ugly*, it wasn't made for an "above average" woman because it has more bumps than I do. When I finally wriggle my oversized boobs into it, I see Nan is right. Some things are sized differently and this thing definitely is one of those things. Thank God for small miracles.

When I come out from the change room Nan is in the main aisle talking to Victoria and Rachel. I turn away hoping they didn't see me come out.

"BJ!" Nan waves. Oh great. No chance of not being seen now. She turns to Victoria and Rachel. "Dis is my granddaughter. Do you know her?"

They look at me, smile, and nod. Oh great; in about ten minutes, my name and pic will be in the high school's paper on the BURN page of the week.

"BJ," Nan comes up to me holding a black dress. "Dees girls were just saying dis one I picked out is really beautiful." I grab the dress and race back into the change room.

The dress is nice. Plain black, kind of low-cut but not so low-cut my boobs are falling out. Tight fitting but not so tight it shows every roll and I can't breathe. And it looks good. It looks *really* good. It's perfect. I pull it off, get dressed, and walk out.

"It doesn't fit, Nan. Can we just go home? I'm kind of tired and nothing here fits me right anyway."

Nan sighs and puts her arm around my shoulder. "Sure, BJ, we can go home."

I don't know what hurts more—the look in Nan's eyes when I told her I wanted to go home, or leaving the perfect dress behind because it was from Target and my Nan picked it out.

* * * *

I want to be at the dance as much as an innocent man wants to be sitting in an electric chair, but I figure if I'm filming Alex's band playing at least I don't have to explain to anyone why no one bothered to ask me to dance.

Rick staggers in—trashed. He throws an empty glass on stage missing everyone and yells, "Get off the stage, faggot! You don't belong there."

People boo at him as he throws another glass, making the band stop playing as they dodge it. He yells something else as two bouncers drag him out of the place but no one can hear what he says over the booing crowd. As he passes me he flips me off but I just smile, wave goodbye, and go back to filming again.

When I zoom in on the band I see Rachel and Victoria in front of the stage. They stare up at Alex, and flirt every time he looks down at them. I bite my bottom lip and swallow. Even though they were mean to me at the beach, I wish I could be like them, ignoring the boys begging for a dance, so I can flirt with someone else.

* * * *

Back home I look at the clips I shot to check to see if there's something I can use for the doc. But seeing all those girls with their arms wrapped around their partners like morning glories hold a fence just makes me feel like a weed in their gardens.

Sunny jumps on my bed and rubs her head into my stomach. I pick her up and cuddle her to my face. "At least you still love me."

Dad knocks and pokes his head inside my door. "Hope you didn't break too many hearts tonight," he goes.

"Only my own," I tell him.

He comes in all the way. "You okay?"

"Yeah." I put Sunny back on the bed.

Dad comes and hugs me. "Feel like a sundae?"

"Yeah." I put away my cam. "Yeah, a sundae would be good."

Even a weed wouldn't turn down one of Dad's sundaes.

Alex's Journal

Giving In

Jen gives me her
"Everything will be okay" look,
as I sneak past Dad
in the kitchen.

She doesn't know the half of it,
but it's good to know
she cares;
I'm even left thinking
it might be easier
to give up, and just be
what Dad wants
me to be.

But then I wonder if I'll even be
good enough for him
once I'm trapped in a life
not my own.

BJ

*As you grow, you learn that everything in
life has its own place, and you learn to stay
in yours.*

When Rachel and Victoria drive by my bus stop
and ask if I want a ride, I turn up my MP3 and play
like I don't hear their calls. When the bus pulls up,
I rush onto it and sit in the front seat. Even though
I want to slide into the back of Victoria's car and
feel like I did when we were laughing in the garage,
I pretend not to see them. Everyone knows girls
like me aren't supposed to sit by girls like them.

* * * *

"I don't want to sit next to BJ when we have our
pictures taken." Steffie Thompson cries.

Mrs. Jarvis, our second grade teacher runs
to give her a Kleenex. She's looking at the class

arrangement. "Jeremy, trade places with Steffie, please."

"Nahuh," Jeremy goes. "I ain't sitting beside BJ either."

Mrs. Jarvis looks back at Steffie.

Steffie's face is getting red dots on it because she's blubbering so hard.

"I know," Adam goes, "BJ can just sit out of the class picture—then no one has to sit beside her."

"Yeah," Steffie goes. "She's going to ruin our picture anyway."

I jump off the bench. "I don't want to have my stupid picture taken with you anyway!" I go to stomp out of the room but Mrs. Jarvis grabs my hand.

"That is not an option. You can stand by me."

I stand alone on the other side of Mrs. Jarvis, fold my arms and glare at the camera as the photographer takes the picture.

From then on, if it was picture day at school, I was sick.

Alex's Journal

WTF?
While we're sitting
in the hallway during our spare,
this old friend of David's strolls up
and smacks the back of his head
for nothing.
He says, "Faggots deserve
to be smacked sometimes,"
then just walks away
like nothing happened.

David clenches his teeth
and stares at his book.

Pete sighs and says,
"What the fuck?
Man, what an asshole."

And I try to hide
deeper
inside myself.

BJ

It's easy to be swayed into believing something when you need it to be true.

I almost bump into Rick when I enter the cafeteria.

"Get away from me or I'm going to hork, bitch." He shoves me.

"Barf on your clothes would improve your smell." I brush past him, before I can hear his comeback. Alex isn't at our usual table, so I sit to wait for him.

Rachel and Victoria walk over holding their lunch trays; both have salads and water.

"What do you want?" I stare at my burger and fries to avoid looking at them.

Rachel goes, "Listen, BJ, we're really sorry if you thought we were being mean at the beach. What those guys did to you was terrible. We were barking at them, for being dogs, not at you. Can we eat with you?"

What they say makes sense, and because I want it to be true so bad I shrug and go, "If you want to."

Victoria says, "You missed a great dance the other night."

"I filmed it," I go.

"Oh, sorry, I didn't see you," she goes.

I smiled, thinking she couldn't have seen anything the way her eyes were crazy-glued to Alex's crotch. It gets quiet for a while. I tap my fork onto my fries, and look anywhere but at them.

"Did you wear that black dress?" Rachel says so suddenly, I jump.

"I didn't buy it."

"Oh." Rachel pouts. "I thought it was cute,"

"Listen, BJ," Victoria goes, "we're going shopping later. We thought you might want to join us."

"You want me to go shopping—with you?" I ask.

"Yeah." Victoria looks at Rachel and smiles. "We have a lot of fun when we hang with you. You know, with all those funny stories you read and tell everyone about. And maybe we can help you choose some clothes, to make you fit in with the other girls more. That way, maybe the guys won't bug you as much."

I'm not sure if this is all a trick, and maybe I shouldn't go. But they seem like they aren't playing with me, and no one found out about my shopping with Nan so they couldn't be that bad. Maybe they really do want to be friends, and the only thing I've ever really wanted was to fit in with all the other girls. Besides, if things get ugly, Victoria and Rachel are both so supermodel skinny, I could just turn on one of the big fans in the mall and blow them away.

Alex's Journal

Skipping

David and I skip school
and head to the beach.

We take our acoustic guitars
and play around with some new
melodies and lyrics.

He's singing the words to
a song I wrote and I play.

His voice fills me up
like a couple of burgers,
but it doesn't
make me feel
like upchucking
afterwards.

BJ

You've got a problem when your entire existence hangs off a text message.

I'm sitting in English texting Alex because he didn't answer his phone earlier and I can't call him right now. Sometimes, when I try to call, and he doesn't answer, I think he's avoiding me.

And sometimes, when that happens, I think I don't have any friends, and that Alex and the band just let me hang around because they're too nice to kick me out.

And sometimes, when that happens, I go up into my room and drown myself in the old videos Dad shot of me and Alex playing when we were small.

And sometimes, when that happens, I wish we could have stayed small forever.

But as I sit here in English, Alex text messages back and tells me he's at the beach practicing with

David and my mind relaxes enough I can get back to reading *To Kill a Mockingbird*.

Alex's Journal

Family

After school,
I try to get hold of BJ
to film our practice,
but she's got her phone off.
So David, Pete, and I practice
without her.

Jacob comes in to watch.
I let him play my electric guitar,
and Pete tries to accompany him
on the drums.
Then David screams in
some inaudible lyrics.

They are making so much noise,
Dad comes in to see
why we sound so bad.
And he sees Jacob grinning

and jumping around, swinging my guitar,
and doing a perfect imitation
of me.
Except the guitar is bigger
than him.

Dad smiles at me,
and puts his arm around my shoulder,
then sits beside me
to watch.

And by the time Jacob gets to the end of his song,
Dad and I are laughing so hard
we both fall off our stools.
And that makes Jacob jump on us
and laugh too.

Right then,
I feel like everything
is the same as it always has been.

But it's not.

BJ

One is easily intimidated by perfection.

At the mall, we hit the expensive stores. The sales-clerks jump all over Victoria and Rachel as soon as they walk in. No doubt because of their perfect hair and their bodies that fit perfectly into their $400 outfits. Even though I walk in with Victoria and Rachel, I'm totally ignored, probably because of my scraggly hair and extra large sized body that fits perfectly into my $7.99 pair of baggy track pants and $2.00 secondhand shirt.

When I look through a rack of clothes, I notice the security camera focusing on me, so I walk to the rack where Victoria and Rachel are standing.

"What's your size?" Rachel holds up a blouse. It's pink, very short, cut close to the body, and so see-through you wouldn't think there'd be enough material in it to make it worth the $60 marked on a huge, red sale sticker flapping from its sleeve.

"I don't think that will fit." I say. "My boobs are slightly bigger than the 'A' cup."

Rachel chokes down a laugh. "Right."

I try not to look at the price tags on the rest of the clothes, but I know Rachel and Victoria see me passing up the pricey clothes. They just buy whatever they like, but my wallet isn't as thick as theirs and it's hard for me to spend that much money on stuff I don't really need.

When I get back to the car, I add up all the receipts in my head and figure at least I'll be in style when they bury my body if my father finds out I spent this much of my college money.

✶ ✶ ✶ ✶

I'm about thirteen and I go up and sit on the arm of Dad's chair. "I want to be a producer when I grow up."

"Is that so?" Dad asks.

"Yeah," I tell him.

"You need to go to college for that."

"I know," I say.

"You going to save your money?"

"Yeah."

"Good," he smiles and pats me on the back. "Tell you what. If you save your money for college I'll pay for half."

"Do you have half?" I ask.

"Not now, but I'll save it," he tells me.

The next day I got my first job delivering papers and Dad started putting some of every paycheck in the bank for my college fund.

Alex's Journal

Opinions

Dad found out
I skipped school to hang
with David.
He slaps me upside my head,
and says "What were you thinking?
David prances around like
some kind of faggot.
You can't be seen hanging
around him
anymore."

He says, "If you do,
people might think
you're a faggot too.
That would be
social suicide."

Dad is so worried about
what other people think
he forgets to give a damn
about what I think.

BJ

*Having a lot of money doesn't make you a
better person, but it sure would be nice.*

Victoria pulls her Beemer into a three-car unat-
tached garage bigger than my house. I grab my
bags and my cam and walk with her and Rachel
past the golf-green lawn and up the walkway to
her house.

A short woman wearing a uniform I didn't
think people actually wore anywhere but in the
movies opens the door for us. We enter a hallway
probably bigger than my entire house. Okay, maybe
not so big but pretty close. There's a crystal chande-
lier on the ceiling. When the sunlight from the window shines on it, it throws rainbows around the
room. They dance over the marble floor.

I step out of my shoes but Rachel just walks in.
I slide my feet back inside hoping they didn't
notice I took them off in the first place.

"Rosita, can you bring some cold drinks up to my room in about a half hour?" Victoria asks the woman.

Rosita nods and hurries into another large room that holds a grand piano and then disappears into another room. I follow Victoria and Rachel up the plush carpeted staircase and down a long hallway full of family portraits. They taunt me with their perfectness; I stare as I walk past one of an ancient man with an accusing glare. It's as if he's telling me I don't belong in this house and to go away. He gives me the creeps. I turn away from him and bump into Rachel who had stopped in front of Victoria's door.

"Sorry," I say.

"S'okay." She looks at Mr. Ancient. "That one makes my skin crawl too."

Victoria has more electronics in her room than I have in my whole house, and for a moment I'm afraid to step in and get a high radiation dose, but the big screen plasma TV pressed against the wall on the other side of the room hypnotizes me and pulls me in like a zombie. *Movies.*

I hook up my cam to her TV and film her and Rachel as they model their new clothes around the room.

After, Rosita brings us low fat milk shakes and we play pool in the games room. While we're hanging around together, even though I don't fully trust them, I get so caught up in trying to be like them, I forget about the blotch that makes me so different.

Alex's Journal

Everything I Want

In the café it's dark
and David and I grab a booth
in the corner.

We talk about school,
friends, fathers,
and music.

In the café it's dark,
but I can still see
David's eyes light up when he laughs
and I wonder if he sees mine light up too.

BJ

There's nothing like the feeling when you can finally one-up someone who has beat you down.

Back home, I stare into the mirror and pat the cover-up Rachel helped me pick out over my birthmark. I must use one eighth of the stick, trying to cover the whole blotch, but when I'm done I can hardly see it.

"BJ?" Dad bangs on the door. "You almost done?"

I open the door.

Dad raises his eyebrows, then blinks. He touches my chin and looks in my eyes. "You look more and more like your mother every day." He sighs and walks past me. "She was beautiful, but I think you're prettier."

He closes the door, leaving me feeling like I just stuck it to my mother.

* * * *

I'm little and I'm in the park with Mommy. We're all alone and she's pushing me on the swing. Then two other little girls come with their mothers. Mommy stops pushing me on the swing and sits on the bench. Now more people come to play and Mommy is watching one of the other little girls and isn't paying attention to me. I go sit next to Mommy and ask her if she brought us any snacks. She plays like she doesn't see or hear me. She's just watching the other girls, so I go play with them and maybe she will see me too.

I'm having fun playing that we're living in a castle and we're all princesses but then Mommy comes. She smiles at the other little girls and goes, "You two don't have to play with BJ." She pulls me away and whispers, "Stop bothering the other girls. You can't be a princess with them. You don't look like one."

Alex's Journal

Losing Myself

I have a date with Emily tonight.
While we're at the movies
I'm more interested in what's on the screen
than making out with her in the dark theater
but I do it because that's what I'm
supposed to want to do.

But her kisses and advances
leave me
empty.

The longer I pretend they don't
the more I feel like
I'm losing
myself.

BJ

Silence between best friends is comforting, but silence after a disagreement can rip you apart.

Alex stands with me in the line at McD's. He's talking about harmony or something and how great a singer David is, but I can't hear anything over the growling of my stomach.

I stare at the menu and my mouth waters.

"Can I help you?" the kid goes.

"Gar sal and a ter, ple." The words get caught in my throat.

"Beg your pardon?" she asks.

I clear my throat. "Can I have a garden salad and a water, please?"

"You feeling okay?" Alex asks.

"I'm on a diet."

"*You* are?"

"Yeah, so what? I want to lose some weight. Is

that okay with you?" I snap and glare at his Big Mac meal. My stomach rumbles again.

"Fine," he goes. "But why? You're not even fat."

"Other people think I'm fat."

"Like who? Victoria and Rachel?" he snaps back.

"Yeah, maybe, and maybe it's everyone else too. Maybe I just want to be more like them—okay?"

He looks at me like I've got two heads and says, "I don't understand why you'd want to be like them."

"You'll never understand, Alex. Not only are you a guy, you're perfect like them."

Right after I say it, I see something in Alex's eyes I've never seen before—doubt. He looks away and, for the first time, the silence between us is uncomfortable.

Alex's Journal

Rocks

BJ has always been
a rock.
She has never been
afraid to be herself.
And now she's forgetting
who she is.

And I'm no longer sure
of who I am.

So with both of us
trying to be
something else
for someone else,
who's left
to be the
Rock?

BJ

Making up with your best friend is the closest place you can get to heaven.

Later, I sit in Alex's garage as he practices his guitar.

He puts the guitar down, and looks deep into my eyes. "BJ," he says. "Be careful with Rachel and Victoria, okay? Girls like them have hidden agendas, and I don't ever want to see you hurt." He leans over and hugs me.

For a short time I know he's right, and I want to just stay safe, alone with him, in the garage.

Alex's Journal

Understanding

I'm exploding inside.
I need to talk to someone
but BJ is always out
with the girls.

I call David, instead.
He's a very good listener.
He understands me.

BJ

Growing apart can freeze your insides like a
winter breeze rushing through an open door.

When I sit with them for lunch, Alex, David, and Pete are engrossed in a conversation about one of their songs that I've never heard before.

David is humming the chords he wants Alex to play on his guitar. Alex's eyes light up as David hums and Pete closes his eyes and taps on the table with his fork and knife.

None of them look up or say hello, and I feel like I'm left outside knocking on a frosted glass window, but no one is letting me in.

Alex's Journal

Scared

There's an empty
space
deep inside me
where no one else
can go.

But when I'm alone
with David
that space
fills up.
And that

scares me.

BJ

Finally being accepted by your peers can drive you crazy.

God, I can't believe I said I'd do this. I'm staring into my closet trying to choose my outfits. A sleep-over at Rachel's? I've never slept over at another girl's house before. What the hell do people do at these things anyway?

My cam is already in my backpack. Guess I need pjs. I pull a raggedy old shirt of my dad's out of my drawer and throw it into my pack. God, what am I thinking—this is a sleepover with Rachel and Victoria, I can't wear that! I pull the shirt back out of my pack and grab the satin pjs my Nan gave me last year. Shit, I'll freeze in these.

What do people *wear* at sleepovers?

I throw the satin pjs in the pack along with a not so raggedy shirt and a pair of sweats.

Hairbrush, toothbrush, makeup. Do I need some kind of a facial mask? People in the movies always do that facial mask thing. I throw in a tube of peel-off mask. Are we going to sing songs like they did in that movie *Grease*? That's an ancient movie . . . probably not. I throw in my MP3 anyway. Cell phone. Pack of cards—just in case.

Oh man . . . what if I get it while I'm there? I throw in a box of tampons. I shouldn't get it. I take them out. But what if? I throw them back in.

Back to the closet. Clothes for tomorrow. Weather? Supposed to be nice and warm. I throw in a skirt and a blouse I bought with the girls. Might be too cold. I pull them out and throw in jeans and a sweater. Might be too hot . . . shit!

I stuff everything I bought that day at the mall in my bag plus some clothes I already had. Do I need to pack food? I look at my bag. No room for food. Besides, Victoria and Rachel don't eat anyway. Breath? I don't want to stink up the tent. I put in a pack of gum.

Shit! A tent! Do I need something to sleep on? Flashlight? Blankets? I cram the flashlight into the pack and stuff a sleeping bag through the arm straps. That should be good. I pick up my pack. Rip! The bottom falls out.

"*Shit!* . . ." I stand staring at it in disbelief. Why me?

"*Dad!*"

* * * *

Outside Rachel's house we line our sleeping bags on the tent floor. I set my cam up so I can film everything and remember this night. Then crawl inside my sleeping bag, stare at the roof of the tent, and smile. Right now, if the world ended I know I'd die feeling alive.

"You want to hear my weird news?" I ask, remembering what I read this morning.

"Yeah!" they go at the same time.

"Well, apparently scientists have invented a new material that a closeted gay person can make clothes out of to prevent other people from guessing he's gay."

"You're kidding?"

"Nope. It blocks out the sixth sense that some people have for picking out gay people. It costs about fifty bucks a yard."

"Weird! Who'd actually pay fifty bucks for that? Like it'd really work." Rachel laughs.

"Really," I go.

"Maybe some big celebrities or something," Victoria says.

"Nah, they don't really care if people know they're gay," Rachel says.

"Yeah," I go. "Politicians would though."

"Those guys would for sure. I bet the mayor is gay," Rachel tells us.

"He's gay. No doubt about it," I say. We're quiet for a bit.

Suddenly, Rachel goes, "You've been best friends with Alex for a long time, right?"

"I suppose so." I shift my pillow beneath my head. "We've been best friends since we were eight."

"Do you want to be more than friends?" Victoria asks. "He's really hot. If he were my best friend, I would want to jump him."

I shrug. "I never really thought about him like that." I remember back to last week when Alex held me close in the garage, and I look away from Victoria's accusing glance, because I'm afraid she can read my real thoughts.

"Really?" Rachel goes, "I figured you'd have some feelings for him."

"I do," I tell them. "I love Alex. He's my best friend. We tell each other everything."

Victoria and Rachel sit up, look at each other, and grin. We don't say anything else for a while.

"Do you know who he likes?" Victoria asks.

"No, we never talk about that," I say.

"I thought you talked about everything." Victoria frowns and gives Rachel a look of desperation and I'm thinking she likes Alex and wants me to tell her he likes her too.

"Well, not that. I wish I could tell you, but really, Alex is too busy with his music to think about girls," I tell them.

Rachel rolls her eyes and looks at me. "Guys always think about girls. I always see him writing in a journal. Have you ever read it?"

"His journal?" I sit up and glare at her.

"Yes, have you read his journal?" Victoria says.

"No, I don't read it," I go. "Those are his private thoughts."

"But you're his best friend," Rachel says. "I thought you knew everything about each other— so why don't you know what's in his journal?"

"Right," Victoria goes. "Rachel and I let each other read our diaries all the time."

I shrug. They watch me and I twist the edge of my sleeping bag until it's a big glob of material and the stuffing is bunched into a huge ball.

"I think you should read it," Rachel says. "Maybe he doesn't think you're a great friend after all. I bet he has some terrible stuff written in there about you."

I scrunch deeper into my sleeping bag, trying to hide away from their words and the words in all those anonymous notes that haunt my mind. "That's not true. Alex and I are best friends. He wouldn't write stuff like that about me. He just wouldn't. I know Alex. He doesn't do stuff like that. He's not that kind of person."

"Okay, BJ. You know him more than we do, but I just don't see what other reason he could have for not letting you read it," Victoria says. "He's got to be writing about you in there—maybe good stuff, maybe not. You'll never know unless you read it."

"Next time you're with him and he leaves it laying around, read it," Rachel tells me, "or better yet, take it. That way you can take your time and read it where you won't get caught—like the girls' locker room."

"BJ, you can't let him keep secrets from you like that. It's not right. That's not real friendship. Rachel and I tell each other everything." Victoria fluffs up her pillow and leans back. "It's just not right what he's doing."

Alex wouldn't write anything bad about me. He just wouldn't. I shift my sleeping bag around again, wrapping it even tighter around me like a hug. I wish I were home watching a late night movie with Dad, instead of lying in a tent where accusations of a failing friendship fly through the silent night air.

Alex's Journal

Deserted

I feel like I've been
deserted
by my best friend.
I'm so confused
about everything,
my father,
my music,
and my feelings
for David.

I wish more than anything
I could change.
But I tried
and I can't.

I need to talk to BJ,
because she knows
all about being different.

And she knows
about being strong.
And I know she can teach me.

But right now,
she doesn't have time
for me and I'm
dying inside.

BJ

When you're told something over and over again, it will eventually burrow itself into your mind and distort your point of view so it becomes real to you.

Sitting in Alex's garage I feel dissed. I have no idea what the guys are talking about anymore, and today they're ignoring me altogether. Everything in my head is messed up and I'm afraid, all my thoughts about our friendship dissolving are true, and I feel like a little kid who just learned Santa isn't real.

I wonder if everyone is right and Alex just pitied me all along. He's the type of guy to be friends with someone just because no one else wants to be. Now that I have other friends, I no longer need to be pitied. But I need to know for sure.

When Alex puts his journal down next to me and turns around to grab his guitar, I pick the journal up and slip it into my bag.

Later, when the guys go home and I'm left alone with Alex, he searches like a maniac. "Have you seen my journal?"

I swallow and look away. "Nope," I say. "I'm sure it's around." I want to give him back the journal, but I'm afraid he'll be mad at me for taking it in the first place. So I clutch my bag closer and say, "I'd help you look, but I have to go."

Alex looks at me like a scared animal in the headlights of a car. But I just slide off the stool and leave him alone in the garage.

PART TWO

Barbara Jean Belanger

Expose an enemy and you can live free of guilt, as that's what society expects; expose a friend and you will be consumed by guilt for all eternity.

I skip first period and sit alone on the bench in the girls' locker room. I pull the journal out of my bag. Its cover is smooth under my hand. I swallow the lump growing in my throat. I shouldn't have this. It's Alex's and it's private.

One entry won't hurt though. I open to the first page and read, but it's addicting and like eating a bag of potato chips you can't just stop with one, so I keep reading.

When I read the part where Alex says he can't breathe without me, I know I should put the book back into my bag and never pull it out again. But there are so many things about Alex I don't know, that I think I should know. So I keep reading.

By the time I reach the end, I'm empty inside because I know I'm the one who stabbed her best friend in the back.

* * * *

I'm face down, drowning in the guilt that glued me to the bench I lie on.

I don't understand how I could have been so stupid to believe my best friend didn't really like me—stupid to believe Victoria and Rachel over him. And I was stupid and selfish not to see that he needed me.

All those signals. All the times he tried to sit me down to tell me. All that time thinking it was all about me—when it was about him. He needed me to be there to understand, and I wasn't. I'm such a loser. I don't deserve him.

I hear someone come in the locker room. They walk closer but I don't move. I just lie there, unable to face anyone, knowing I'm everything my mother told me I was.

They stop beside me. I hear whispers, but can't understand them—it all sounds like a foreign language. I feel a breeze against my arm. Then they move farther and farther away until I can no longer hear them.

The bell rings and classes change. At one point there are more people in the room but I don't move. Someone pokes me—probably to make sure I'm still alive—so I groan, "Leave me alone."

After several class changes it occurs to me that Alex never has to know I took the journal. I can just put it back in the garage. I can pretend I don't know everything I know, because to me it doesn't matter anyway. To me, Alex will always be Alex and I will always love him for him. So I sit up but when I go to grab the journal off the floor—it's gone.

My heart races as I run out of the locker room. I push through the crowd of kids huddled in the hallway.

A little way down the hall someone's cell rings. "Oh my God! You're kidding, right?" the girl answering it goes. "Sick!" She hangs up the phone. She leans over and whispers to her friends.

"Can't be true," some guy says as I get closer to the cafeteria.

"It's true," someone else tells him.

"No way," another kid goes. I don't stick around long enough to hear what they're talking about.

"Good grab!" someone yells as I pass—must have dropped something and his friend caught it.

I run into a girl who is in the process of texting a friend.

"Sorry!" I holler back but keep moving through the blurred faces searching for the only one that matters.

"There she is," someone behind me says but I can't stop to see who it was, or who he was waiting for. I have to find Alex. I have to let him know someone has his journal. I'll tell him I found it and then someone else took it from me. I won't tell him I read it, I'll just tell him . . .

Oh, good—Alex is in the cafeteria surrounded by our friends. He sees me, and waves; then grabs for his cell. Mine rings at the same time. I answer and step forward.

"I love Alex." I hear over the phone. I stop. It's me talking. I think back to where I said it—Victoria's tent. They must have taped our conversation.

I look up and Alex is staring at me from across the room—like he hears it too. It's a three-way call.

"I mean, I used to love Alex but I read his journal. He thinks we're best friends, but we aren't. Not anymore—I don't even like him. He's gay. It says in his journal. I'll let you read it too. I can get it for you." It's me talking again but I never said that. They must have broken up all of our conversations from that night and pieced them back together.

I see Alex, his face white as he holds his cell close to his ear and leans against a chair. He's staring at me with his jaw hitting the floor.

I can't look away.

He's staring at me with tears in his eyes.

I want to run to him and tell him I never said those things—would never say them. But I'm frozen, wondering why this is happening. Do they really hate me this much?

I glance around. Do they all hate me because of the way I look? Everyone is staring at me. They're whispering and pointing and I finally understand the broken conversations in the hallway—that kid yelling, "Nice grab." I finally understand everything. My legs go weak. Heat rushes up my neck and spreads across my face and I know that no matter what I do or say now—everyone knows.

It's not me they hate anymore. It's Alex—and it's all my fault.

* * * *

The mirror in front of me is reflecting a face I
don't recognize—the face of someone plastic, selfish, and stupid.

The face of someone who wears makeup to
cover up the

large

ugly

blotch

on the side of that face.

I stand here, in front of the mirror, looking at
the blotch and hearing all the voices in my past
that blotch represents.

I hear my mother yell at me and call me ugly
just before she left.

I hear the kids in grade two say I'm going to
ruin our class picture.

I hear the voices of the bullies chanting, "Ugly!
Ugly!"

I hear the voices of the girls in high school
who left those notes.

I hear the voices of Victoria and Rachel telling
me to take Alex's journal.

I hear Alex's voice saying why?

I would do anything to make those voices go away but the more I try the louder they get. The only way to smother those voices is to remove what's causing them to scream.

I take the wire hairbrush out of my backpack. I bring that wire brush up to my face, up to my blotch. And I try to scrape that blotch off the face of the girl I no longer recognize.

* * * *

Inside our school,
inside the girl's locker room,
inside one of the shower stalls,
I lie bleeding into the puddles
of water left on the floor by all those
perfect girls.

* * * *

But I don't get up, because inside,
I'm Dead.

* * * *

The glare from the window hurts my eyes and I squint. I'm tucked tight in a bed. The smell of antiseptic makes me so dizzy I feel like upchucking.

There's a crack in the ceiling—or a wire running across it—or something. I'm not sure. I can't see clearly. I try to rub my eyes, but can't move my hands. I jerk them again but they're tied to something.

Shit! Where the hell am I? I'm tied up and drugged. I panic, jerking my hands away from the bed again. I have to get loose but it's no use. All I'm doing is making myself tired. I try to call out but my throat is dry and my "help . . ." just comes out a gurgle.

"They tied your hands because you kept trying to scratch off your face in your sleep," someone goes from beside me.

I turn my head towards the voice. There's this girl sitting on the bed next to mine. Her blonde hair is cut uneven to her scalp, jaggedly, like someone did it with a knife. She's propped up with several pillows and she's using the remote control in her bandaged hand to flick the TV channels.

After a few minutes of flicking she looks away from the TV and at me, "Welcome to the psych ward, my name is Amanda, and I'll be your temporary nutcase of a tour guide." She snorts, turns away, and flicks the channels again.

I clear my throat. "Psych ward?" I whisper her words. "How?"

"You ripped off half your face and part of your neck," she says. "Where else do you think they'd put you?"

★ ★ ★ ★

I sit, slumped in a metal folding chair, in the middle of a room full of kids, all slumped in metal folding chairs. All of us here because we hurt ourselves, and we can't leave until everyone believes we won't do it again.

The kids don't look at my face, my bandages, or me, and I don't look at their faces, their bandages, or them. Instead, everyone just fixes their eyes on the floor. It's as if everyone else sees the same squiggly things crawling over the floor that I see. They look like worms—glowing worms. I want to look up, away from the crawling things. I want to look at the kids sitting in the circle, but I'm too tired. My head is heavy. My mind is heavy.

Even the air around me is heavy-heavy and crawl-ing with glowing worms.

"Who wants to begin today?" Doc West, our shrink, asks the group.

I sit—too tired to say anything—and wait for someone else to begin, but no one is volunteering. Someone shifts and the vinyl on their chair makes a farting noise, breaking the silence. A few kids chuckle, but then everything goes silent again.

"Barbara? You want to begin?" Doc asks. "Can you tell us about yourself?"

At first I wonder who he's talking to; then I realize it's me. So I go, "It's BJ and I'm tired."

"That's a start," Doc says. "Anything else?"

"No."

A piercing scream splits the air and a nurse runs down the corridor. Wide-eyed, some of the group kids rush to look down the hall.

I'm too tired to look.

* * * *

My head is clearing and I'm getting into the soap opera Amanda is watching. Some dude just divorced his wife when he found out she was really his sister by their estranged father. The dude's not upset about it because he's really in love with the woman he thought was his sister but turned out not to be because the guy he thought was his father was not really his father.

A female nurse with a hairy upper lip is suddenly standing in front of the TV.

"Hey, if I didn't want to see the TV I'd stand in the hallway." I try to shoo her away but Hairy Lip snarls and moves closer.

"Read this and sign it." She hands me a clipboard with a paper attached.

"Oh, man." I roll my eyes. I don't have to read it. It's the same thing they got me to read and sign for the last four days.

* * * *

No-Suicide Contract
I, Barbara Jean Belanger, agree that I will not harm myself or attempt suicide in any way.

If ever I am ever suicidal:
1) I will discuss my feelings with a caring and supportive person.

2) I will call 911 if I am in danger of harming myself.

3) I will notify Dr. West if I have suicidal thoughts.

* * * *

I sign it and hand it back.

Hairy Lip hands me a pill and a glass of water. "This will make you feel better."

"Sure it will," I go. I swallow the pill and she checks inside my mouth to make sure it's gone, then turns to Amanda.

"Read this and sign it."

"Later, my soap is on," Amanda goes.

"Read this and sign it," the nurse says again. She pushes the clipboard towards Amanda, who looks up disgusted but takes the board and scribbles her name on it.

"I will not hurt myself again," she exaggerates her words as she says them. The nurse makes sure she swallows her pill then turns away to stalk her next victim.

I sit and try to get back into the soap, but the meds make my head fog up and the glowing, wiggly things come back. Soon I'm too tired to understand what any of the actors is saying and I forget what was going on anyway, and seeing the actor on TV makes me remember the actor who made his nose disappear with that new makeup, and that makes me remember the fight with Rick, and how he acted with David, and how Rick was a friend, but now he's not, and how I was Alex's friend too, and how he couldn't breathe without me, but now I'm not and he can't breathe, and how Alex probably doesn't have many friends left, because everyone knows he's gay, and how it's all my fault, and how I have to get out of here and tell Alex I never said those things, and how I'm too tired right now to do anything, and how the nurse said this medicine will make me feel better, but how it doesn't make me feel better, it just makes me forget what I was just thinking, so I watch the actors on TV but don't understand anything they are saying because this medicine makes me tired, but the actor on TV makes me remember about the actor who made his nose disappear and that makes me think of Rick, and he makes me think of Alex, and that makes me think of how I have to get out of here, but I don't remember why.

* * * *

Amanda eats with me. She doesn't stare at my blotch or my scar. She doesn't ask questions like everyone else. She just sits and eats with me, and when some kid walks by us and calls me ugly, Amanda makes sure the guards aren't looking then slams the kid in the face. "Don't call my friends nothing but their name."

Amanda doesn't take shit from no one and I like that about her.

* * * *

They switched my meds so now my head's not so foggy and I set up my own chair for group therapy.

"Who's going to start?" Doc asks.

When no one volunteers, he says, "Amanda?"

Amanda shrugs, "Whatever." She looks around. "I was going out with Jeff for three years. I gave him everything, and he dumped me for some bimbo in the middle of all our friends while we were partying at the beach. I got mad and wanted to make him pay for dumping me like that. So in front of everyone, I smashed open a bottle and used the jagged edge to cut off all my hair. And that landed me in here." She tries to hide her wrists behind her back.

"Guess you didn't stop with your hair, huh?" some boy with red hair and a face full of zits goes.

"Shut the fuck up!" Amanda stands and rushes him.

Doc grabs her shoulder gently and makes her sit back down. "In this room we respect others' safety."

"Sylvie?" Doc says to a quiet girl.

Sylvie looks up, pale-faced. Her blue eyes are sunken—hollow, like she's already dead. She looks at Doc and starts to shake. I don't mean a little shake. I mean major convulsions that make Doc stand up real quick and rush to her, and just when I think she's about to collapse she speaks instead.

"I hate my brother. I hate his warty hands. I hate the way he smells, the way he comes into my room every day." Her voice gets louder. "I hate the way he stares. I hate the way he goes out of his way to pick a lock and follow me into a room. I hate that he still comes after me when I yell, 'Leave me alone!' I hate being in the house alone with him. I hate him! And the only way to get away was to down a bottle of pills and just hoped I'd die. I didn't die

BUT
I
STILL
JUST
WANT
TO
DIE!"

* * * *

"Well, there's a fast way to kill a group therapy session and get us free time," Amanda says as we head back to our room.

"Yeah, but then you end up with a one on one with Doc," I tell her. "I'd rather sit and say nothing in group."

"True," she goes. "Why did you try to off yourself?"

"I didn't," I tell her.

"You did too," this tall, bony kid from group named Jordan goes. "I go to your school. I was there. I heard the tape of you saying you were going to give them Alex's journal."

"So, that doesn't mean dick. I didn't say that shit anyway. It was fixed and I wasn't trying to off myself."

"Like anyone believes you." Jordan snorts.

"Well, you're here too. Maybe you tried to do yourself in but I didn't." I shove him hard against the wall.

He pushes away and plants his feet so I can't knock him again. "I overdosed by mistake. You tried to kill yourself because they humiliated you and your best friend in front of the entire school. Now you don't have any friends left."

"Shut the fuck up!" I spin around and walk away as fast as I can.

Amanda races to catch up. "Shut the fuck up? Am I wearing off on you?"

"Maybe." I smile at her.

"Could have worse people wearing off on you." She wraps her arm over my shoulder. "Listen, don't worry about him. He's an asshole. All guys are assholes. If you weren't trying to kill yourself, what were you doing?"

" I just wanted to get rid of my blotch."

"By scraping it off?" Amanda asks.

"Yeah."

"That was stupid."

"Yeah."

* * * *

"Sign this," Hairy lipped nurse goes.

"Not now. My soap is on," I tell her.

"Sign this."

"Later."

She turns to Amanda. "Sign this."

"My soap is on."

"Sign it."

"No."

Hairy Lip sighs loud. "Sign this!"

"Later."

Hairy Lip makes us take our meds, then bustles out of the room.

"Wonder if she knows what W-A-X spells," I say, and Amanda and I break into hysterics. We get to laughing so much another nurse comes in and checks on us.

* * * *

Dad sits across the table from me. He shifts in his chair and looks down. "Brought you these." He hands me two *Weird World News* magazines. "I figured you'd miss them."

"I do," I go.

"How are you feeling?" He still doesn't look at me.

"Better."

"Good."

I make faces at him but he can't see them because there's no reflection on the table and I just want him to look at me. I plead with him in my mind. Dad, LOOK at me. But he doesn't.

"How's everyone?" I ask.

"Fine.

"Where's Nan?"

"Work."

"Anyone call?" I ask.

"No."

These one-word answers are driving me nuts, so I pick up one of the *Weird* mags and while I'm sitting across the table from my father who can't bear to look at me, I read it silently.

* * * *

"Listen to this," I tell Amanda as I read *Weird*. "Some guy in Asia somewhere had an itchy ear, and he couldn't make it stop itching so he went to see his doctor. Turns out a fly had laid like a million eggs in his ear and they all hatched. There were maggots inside his head."

"Eeww! Talk about an egghead."

Her words remind me of something else and I close the paper not wanting to think about it.

"My dad wouldn't look at me today."

"That's rough." She comes and sits on my bed. "He'll come around. Parents always do. He's probably blaming himself or something. My folks did at first too. I mean, don't most parents blame themselves when something happens to their kids?"

"I suppose so," I go.

She hugs me. "It'll be okay." Her saying it makes me believe it will be.

* * * *

Amanda gets to leave today. She gathers her stuff and shoves it in the bag her friend brought her to take home. "A couple of things I've learned in here. One: to get out—you talk. Tell them bullshit if you have to. Just talk and they'll let you out. Look at Jordan—certified mental but he started talking and he's gone home—right?"

"Absolutely." I nod.

"So start talking, BJ. Get out of this hellhole."

"Okay." I nod again. Right now I don't care if I leave. I don't want to talk to Victoria or Rachel because they're just bitches, and Alex, David, and Pete probably won't want to talk to me because now I'm a bitch too. I have no friends to go back to and it's been two weeks and Dad and Nan still can't look at me.

"Number two," she goes. "This program was all bullshit. Signing a piece of paper saying I won't hurt myself every day for a week isn't going to stop me. If I want to go home and hurt myself again—I will."

"Are you going to?" I ask.

"Pffftttt . . . no." She shoves a book into her bag without looking directly at me. "I just mean if I wanted to—I could. I don't want to. Guys aren't worth the shit they put you through." She avoids looking at me and my stomach turns.

Amanda takes her bag and goes into the washroom.

Then a nurse brings a wheelchair so Amanda can be wheeled out in style. "Where is she?"

I point to the washroom.

The nurse bangs on the door, "You almost ready, darlin'?"

But there is no answer and the silence from the washroom makes me break out in a sweat.

"Amanda?" the nurse goes again.

But there's still no answer, and I want to throw up, but Amanda is in the washroom.

"Amanda?" the nurse's voice has a higher pitch than before. She whips out keys and opens the door. Inside the bathroom, Amanda is sprawled on the floor, her wrists bleeding onto the white floor tiles.

* * * *

I keep thinking about how I felt when Amanda said it was all bullshit. I keep thinking about how her words made my stomach turn. I keep seeing her on the floor. I keep seeing the blood.

All

that

blood.

I keep thinking how she said, "If I want to go home and hurt myself again, I will." I keep thinking and I don't want to think about that anymore.

So I think about something else.

Now, I keep thinking about how Alex said he couldn't breathe without me. I keep thinking about how I stabbed him in the back. I keep thinking about how much I need him. I keep thinking about how much he needed me. I keep thinking of all my blood on the locker room floor. I keep thinking about it and it's making me crazy and I don't want to

THINK

ABOUT

IT.

But I keep thinking, and I don't want to think about it anymore because it's making the air so thick I can't catch my breath. The more I try to stop thinking the thicker the air gets. I'm drowning in thick air and it's making me crazy.

The voices of my mother, of all those kids at school, of Alex—they're screaming at me again. The voices in my head keep telling me I'm worthless. They tell me I don't deserve to live for what

I've done. You don't stab a friend in the back. You just don't.

Those voices are getting louder and louder. I turn up the soap on TV to drown them all out, but it doesn't work. I turn it full blast so it echoes around the room.

I'm watching that soap and it's making me mad, and the actors are making me mad because it's all so fake. It's making me so mad—it's not funny.

I want to scream and throw things. It's making me that mad. So I throw the remote control straight into the TV. The actors poof with an explosion of shattering glass. And there is broken glass all over the floor. I'm so mad at the soap I want to just pick up that glass and slice my wrists and stop the voices and stop THINKING. And I want to just disappear for a while like Raven did on the soap. But I don't because that soap made me so mad.

People don't come back from the dead like Raven did. They don't just dig themselves out of the grave after they killed themselves and come back with a new face two years later. There are no fake doubles to say that's who everyone buried.

There are no "I love yous" and "I forgive yous," even though you lied to everyone. There are no "I don't mind that I trusted you and you stabbed me in the back." There are no second chances.

In real life there are no second chances to tell people what you need to tell them. No second chances to say sorry.

In real life once you're dead,
you're dead.
There are
NO
SECOND
CHANCES.

It all makes me so mad, I pick up one of those pieces of glass before the nurses rush into the room and I hide that shard in my slipper. They shoo me out of the room so they can clean it up, and when I put my foot into my slipper, the glass cuts my foot but I don't cry.

I can't cry.

Because no one likes a crybaby.

So instead of crying, I smile because the pain makes me feel alive just to feel something other than anger.

*   *   *   *

They move me out of the room completely, thinking it's probably not a good thing for me to stay in there anyhow, but I find myself going back there to think.

Sitting alone in this room with nothing to do but stare at the crack in the ceiling,

I figure, no matter what I did, I would never have been just one of the girls.

I wonder why I ever wanted to be. I was happy just having Alex and the guys. At least with them they'd tell me straight up what was bugging them.

I don't even like the things girls do. They're devious and mean. They trick you just to get what they want. Victoria wanted Alex. She couldn't have him so she destroyed him. Typical girl.

My mother was like that. Always stabbing me in the back. Telling other people shit, like saying I wasn't even her daughter, just so they didn't think there was something wrong with her.

Amanda was like that too. She pulled me in making me believe she was so strong— then offed herself because she wasn't strong enough. I did it to Alex—stabbed him in the back and took his diary. I don't want to be like that.

I'm thinking about that sleepover and about how Rachel and Victoria told me to take his journal. I remember the footage I took at the sleepover. It gives me hope. I know—although I'll have to admit to Alex that I took his journal—I can show him I never said the things he thinks I said. I can show him I never planned on showing his journal to anyone.

But before I can do that, I have to get out of this hell I'm stuck in.

* * * *

I'm sitting in a one-on-one with Dr. West. He's waiting to see if I'm going to say something.

I have to say something. I have to get out. Amanda was right—to get out you talk.

"Do you ever cry?" I ask him.

He takes a deep breath and lets it out like he's relieved. "Sometimes—do you?"

"No. Nobody likes a crybaby."

"Who told you that?"

"My mother. 'Stop crying, no one likes a crybaby,' she said. And she banged my head against the car seat, and called me ugly."

"And then what happened?" he asks.

"She left me alone in the car and went away forever."

"How did that make you feel?"

"How would it make you feel?"

"It doesn't matter how I'd feel. What matters is how it made you feel."

"Like hiding."

"And did you hide?"

"Do you see me?"

He leans forward and looks at me—not the way other people look at me. He actually looks at me—not at all my fat, not at my scar, not at the blotch under the scar. He looks at me, and he smiles. "Yes, I do see you, BJ. I see you."

And then it happens.

I cry.

* * * *

My last evaluation must have proved I'm not crazy, but I'm still crying when I'm packing my stuff to go home. My eyes are so red and puffy from crying I miss the bag's opening when I try to put my slippers inside and they fall onto the floor.

When I pick them up again the shard of glass I put inside slides out and pings against the floor.

I stare at it for a while.

Thinking.

It glitters in the light.

And I think.

Then I pick it up, grab my bag and head to the nurses' station. The nurse looks up and smiles at me. "We're supposed to come and get you. Guess you just can't wait to get out of here."

I place the glass shard on the desk. "You missed one the other day."

The nurse stares at the shard. She blinks, then looks up at me, smiles, and nods. "Thanks, BJ." She hands me the last safety contract I'll ever have to sign. I sign it and give it back, knowing, at least for now, I plan to keep that promise.

★   ★   ★   ★

When I get home and find my cam, I call Alex. I'm sure he knows it's me but he's screening his calls, so I curl up on my bed and cry myself to sleep.

I'm so tired. I don't think I can move, but I overhear Dad and Nan in the next room arguing.

I know they're worried about me, so I drag myself out of bed to go and tell them I'll be fine. But on the way, I pass the mirror and see that even though my face is starting to heal, it still looks like half cooked hamburger.

I gasp. Even though I promised myself I wouldn't hide anymore, I do.

I crawl back under my covers where I stay safe from everyone else, but mostly I go there to stay safe from what I might do if I look again.

* * * *

Nan and Dad stopped arguing and except for the drone of the TV, the house is silent. And I wonder if Alex is home. He won't answer my calls but he can't stop me from going over there. Then I remember Amanda's words, "Guys aren't worth the troubles they put you through." But words can lie. She lied about how she felt. Her actions spoke her truth. Besides, Alex never gave me any troubles. I gave them to him, and I have to apologize.

So even though it makes my insides mash up and flip around until they reach my throat, I force myself out of bed to face the world.

I walk with my camera towards his house. It's only a few blocks but it's sunny and warm and people are out walking. When they stare, I net the butterflies in my stomach and look them straight in their eyes. When I smile at them, they smile back and that gives me enough strength to take another step and soon I'm in front of Alex's garage door.

Alex is inside playing his guitar. Pete and David are with him, so I guess his real friends stuck by him.

He looks up and freezes. He mouths my name but nothing comes out.

I look into his eyes, pleading with him to forgive me but I can't make myself say any words.

Finally David asks, "Why?"

"I didn't." I look down and take a deep breath. "I have to show you . . ." I hold up my cam. Tears fill my eyes and sink into the deep gouges running across my cheek. "I'm sorry, they . . ."

Alex shakes all over.

I want to run to him but my feet won't move. "I'm sorry," I repeat myself. "I'm so sorry. You have to understand." Now I'm shaking too and my feet finally listen to my brain. I put the camera down and run to Alex and grab his arm and I hug it. "Please, I'm sorry. I didn't say those things. I would never. Please, believe me. I can show you."

But he just stands there, all stiff. He pulls his arm away and turns his back on me. "Go home, BJ. Just go home."

PART THREE

ALEX

Three Way

A three way call
usually brings friends together
but when that three way call
involves your best friend
telling someone
your deepest secrets
it makes your whole world
crash down around you.

Liar, Liar

In the cafeteria
Rick says,
"I read your journal.
It explains everything."
He shoves me against the table.
"Faggot!"
I look straight into David's eyes,
and say, "I'm not."

Rick snorts and yells
to everyone,
"Alex Fitzgerald is a fag!"

Standing in front of
all my friends and looking at David
I say, "Faggots disgust me."

In the cafeteria,
a piece of my heart
is ripped out of my chest.
and it leaves with David,
as he walks away.

Hiding Out

Back home,
I hide behind my music.

My father comes in
and says something.

But I don't hear him,
because I'm too involved
in playing away
the world.

So he screams
"Turn it down,
or I'll take away that
damn guitar!"

I jump
and tell him, "Sorry."

I plug in my earphones,
because I know if I don't,
he'll take away
my escape from the real world.
And right now that world is
killing me.

Truths

Someone touches my arm.

I jump, letting go of my guitar.
It crashes to the floor,
and I look up.

Jacob stands in front of me,
holding his guitar and grinning.
He says, "Alex, look what
I learned."

"Don't come up to me like that!
Look what you made me do!"
I yell at him.

He starts crying
and I grab his shoulders
and give him a little shake.
"Don't you ever be like me!"

That scares him even more,
and he bawls harder.

I wrap my arms around him
and hold his head to my chest
and whisper, "I'm sorry, Jacob.
I'm sorry."

I kiss the top of his head,
and I tell him I love him.

I hold him there,
close to me,
letting my tears fall
onto his soft curls.

What BJ Did

Pete races into the garage.
He says, "The girl's volleyball team
just found BJ laying
on the floor in a shower stall
in the girls' locker room
half dead."

Jacob screams,
and Jen rushes in to see
what's wrong,
and he tells her, "BJ's dead."

She looks at me,
distressed.
"Oh, my God."

I tell her, "She's not dead.
Jacob misunderstood.
She's not dead, Jacob."
I hug him hard.
"Everything's okay.
BJ'll be fine.
She'll be just fine,"
I tell him, trying to

convince myself
it's true.

Jen takes a deep breath
and lets it out.
"Thank God."

I look at Pete,
and he understands
not to say anything else,
in front of the kid.

But when Jen and Jacob leave,
he tells me the whole story.

"I guess what comes around
goes around," I say, shrugging it off
like it doesn't bother me but
I'm having a hard time
Breathing.

Missing Parts

There's something burrowing
through my heart leaving
a hole where BJ used to be
and I'm aching
inside.

Walls

Everywhere I look,
are things that remind me of BJ—
A shirt in a store that says, *Bite Me*,
A copy of *Weird World News*,
A girl eating a double burger with fries,
A lady with a video camera.
Especially the cam . . .

And it makes me miss her.

Then I remember what
she did to me,
and anger builds up
inside me like brick walls.

Every day, those walls get
stronger, and soon I feel like
I'm in a vault.

Inside that vault
I feel safe.

Inside that vault,
nothing can hurt me.

Inside that vault,
I don't feel anything.
Inside that vault,
I can't even feel Jacob's hugs for nothing.

I don't like that.

Screening Calls

My phone rings
but when I grab it
I see BJ's number on the display,
so I turn it off.

Pete asks, "Aren't you going to answer?"

"No," I say.
"I don't ever want
to talk to her
again."

School

At school now,
if I say hi,
most kids
don't hi back.

Instead they move away from me like
I have some kind of
contagious disease.

People who were
my friends
don't talk to me
anymore.

Everything I thought
would happen
is happening.
More than anything though,
I'm afraid of what will happen,
if my father ever finds out.

David and Me

David has forgiven me,
but I try not to be
alone with him.
I can't be
alone with him.

But more than anything
I want to be
alone
with
him.

A Never Ending Ride

I'm so torn up
inside.
I'm dizzy all the time.
It's like my world
is a big merry-go-round,
and the only way
to stop spinning is to
fly off.

Broken Friendships

I'm in the garage
playing with the band and suddenly
BJ is right in front of me.
I can't look at her.
If I do, I know I'll forgive her
and right now,
I'm not ready to
forgive.

Best Brother

When the guys leave,
I sit alone in the garage,
and cry.

Jacob comes in and pats my head,
like I'm a dog.
He wipes my cheek
with his little hand,
and says, "Don't cry. It's okay.
I'm here now."
Then he hugs me,
and whispers, "I love you, Alex."

And I wonder how someone
so small
can make me feel
so much better.

BJ's Truth

As I pull Jacob
onto my lap and hug him,
I notice BJ left her camera behind.
I remember she had something to show me.
So I flicked it on
and watched through the display.

I see BJ, Victoria, and Rachel
inside a tent.
I see BJ turn to fluff up her pillow.
I see Rachel pull out a mini recorder,
flick it on and stuff it under her pillow.
I hear their conversations,
about everything.

I hear their conversations,
about my journal,
but nowhere,
do I hear BJ say
anything
I heard her say
over the phone.
And I know
we were both
fucked over.

I'm still mad,
because she took
my journal.

But I know,
that I'm ready
to forgive her.

My Father

During the basketball game,
no one passes me the ball.
During the basketball game,
the coach yells at the team.
During the basketball game,
the team still won't pass to me.
During the basketball game,
the coach pulls me.
During the basketball game,
I look up in the stands,
and sometime,
during the basketball game,
my father left.

Nightmares

Victoria sneers when I walk by her.
She says, "I knew you were a fag,
all along."
She says, "That would explain
a lot of things."
She says, "I read your journal,
then gave it to someone else
during the basketball game."

Then she leaves me standing
in the middle of the hall
with my stomach turning.

In the Garage

In the garage,
my father stands
holding up
my journal.

In the garage
I'm shaking.

In the garage,
my father stands,
blaming my mother.

In the garage,
I'm crying.

In the garage,
my father stands,
forcing his rules.

In the garage,
I'm sorry.
In the garage,
my father stands,
shouting.

In the garage,
I'm begging.

In the garage,
my father stands,
un-accepting.

In the garage,
I'm no longer perfect.

In the garage,
my father
stands,
alone.

Running

Rain spatters
all around me,
soaking me,
as I try to
hide
from it,
and everything else,
under the overpass.

Nowhere to Turn

All I want is to
talk to BJ,
because she always
understood
about my dad and me.

But I still don't know
if I can trust her yet.
So I slide my back
down the cold concrete.
I rest my head
on my knees,
and stay like that
until I fall
asleep.

What I Know

I don't know
if my father
will ever accept
what I am.

I don't know
if my friends
will ever accept
what I am.

I don't know
if I
will ever accept
what I am.

But right now,
I feel so alone,
that I call the only person
I know will
accept me.

I Don't Want to Be

David and I
meet
in my garage.

For a long time,
we just sit quietly.

And then I say,
"Everyone knows now.
My life is over."

David says,
"You're wrong.
Your life is just starting.
Now you can be you,
and you don't have to
pretend anymore."

"But I don't want to be gay," I say.

"No one *wants* to be gay.
It's just the way some of us were made.
We have to learn
to deal with it the best we can."

He puts his arm around my shoulder
and hugs me, like a real friend would.
He sits with me, silent, and lets me cry
about something he understands.

I stay in his arms,
and let the walls
I built around me
fall.

Confrontation

Suddenly Rick is standing
in the garage entrance
with a bunch of other kids.

"I knew it," Rick says.
"I knew it from the moment
you let the fag into the group,
and kicked me out.
You're just like him."

The mob steps forward.
David and I break into a run,
trying to escape through the door,
but we're pinned down.
Rick runs at me,
and throws the first punch.
Then he picks up David's bass
and swings it wildly over David,
and David screams.
He has no way
of getting out of the way.
It hits him in the back,
and I hear a thump.

David doesn't move.

The rest of the group jump
on me.

And soon,
I see BJ by the door.
She's just a blur
through all the fists,
flying at my face.

BJ is tearing into the garage.
BJ is screaming, and pulling at arms
to keep them away
from me.

BJ is yelling,
"That's Alex!"
BJ is screaming over the cries
of the angry mob.
"He's still Alex!"
BJ is clawing at their faces,
trying to get them off of me.
She's screaming,
"He's still the same kid

we all grew up with!
He's still Alex."

As they hit me,
BJ is screaming,
and clawing,
and trying to stop them.

BJ is trying.
But they push her off
and she bangs her head against the drum set
and it crashes down around her
and she doesn't get back up.

And Rick raises the bass again,
but this time,
it's over my head,
and for the first time
in my life,
I am truly
AFRAID . . .

BJ

I'm standing here, in front of God, the priest, and the congregation, trying to give my best friend's eulogy, and all I can think is why, and that's when it hits me.

"There'll always be crap that happens in your life that'll make you wonder what the hell God was thinking when he created humans. What happened to Alex Fitzgerald is one of those things. I can't stop thinking about *WHY* it happened.

"Everyone who knew Alex, even a tiny bit, loved him. He was the type of guy we could just hang out with without worrying about what he thought about us, how he saw us, or what he was going to say about us behind our back.

"Alex was *home* to us and we should have been *home* to him. We should have made him feel like we'd accept him for him — no matter who he was inside. Instead, we placed him high on a podium like he was some kind of God. That was wrong.

Alex was Alex, and that should have been good enough for us. But him not being perfect scared me. It scared all of us. I think it scared him too. Because of that, Alex felt he could never be himself. He felt we wouldn't still love him for him— some of us didn't. We didn't understand him. I think to fully love someone you have to understand them.

"Alex wrote something in his journal: 'I don't know how people can be so consumed with so much hate or fear for something they don't understand that they don't realize what they are doing at the time they are doing it.'

"Well, I don't get it either. I guess we were never meant to get it. More than anything else, Alex's death makes me want to understand the things I'm afraid of—mostly things about myself. Maybe after I understand those things I can learn to fully love myself and then I'll be able to accept and love everyone else. Maybe we should all try to do that. I think that's what Alex would have wanted."

Alma Fullerton was born in Ottawa, Ontario. She spent a year in Germany, where she met her husband, Claude. She now resides in Midland, Ontario, with her husband and two daughters, juggling real life with her passion for literature for youth.